CYCLONES
AND SHADOWS

This edition first published in 2017 by
FREMANTLE PRESS
25 Quarry Street, Fremantle 6160
Western Australia
www.fremantlepress.com.au

Lilli and her Shadow and *Beach Sports Car* were first published as individual titles in 2010; *Lilli and Shadow in Trouble* and *A Cyclone is Coming!* were first published as individual titles in 2013.

Cover design and cover illustration by traceygibbs.com.au.
Printed by McPherson's Printing Group, Australia.

National Library of Australia Cataloguing-in-publication data available.

ISBN 9781925164763 (pbk)

 Government of **Western Australia**
Department of **Culture and the Arts**

Fremantle Press is supported by the State Government through the Department of Culture and the Arts.

CYCLONES
AND SHADOWS

STORIES FROM UP NORTH

LAURA DUDGEON
PAT DUDGEON
SABRINA DUDGEON-SWIFT
DARLENE OXENHAM

 FREMANTLE PRESS

CONTENTS

LiLLi

AND HER

SHADOW

**PAT DUDGEON
AND LAURA DUDGEON**

SAYING GOODBYE

'There won't be any mangoes like this where
you're going, Lilli girl!' said Lilli's grandmother.
She slurped her mango noisily and the yellow
juices ran down her chin. Lilli thought other
people might think her Nan was disgusting,
the slobbery way that she ate mangoes,
pulling them straight from the trees, tearing
the green skin off with her teeth, and biting
into the rich sweet insides. But Lilli liked eating
them that way too. Biting into the skin gave
the mango a wild tang and the juices spurting
everywhere was great fun. This was just one
of the many things she would long for when
her family moved to the city.

'I'll really miss you, Nan!' sighed Lilli. 'I wish we didn't have to go.'

She loved talking and laughing with Nan, sitting together on the old blanket under the big mango tree with the dogs.

'Don't look so sad,' Nan replied. 'You can ring me every day and visit me on the school holidays too!'

Lilli knew that was true, but it just wouldn't be the same.

'Come on,' said Nan, getting up stiffly.

'We'd better get you home. Your mother will be going mad, finishing all that packing on her own.'

Nan passed Lilli the washer she kept specially for mango clean ups. Lilli wiped her face and looked around Nan's beautiful garden one last time.

'We'll call in at your Uncle Bernie's house on the way,' Nan said. 'He wants to say goodbye to you and so do your cousins.'

Lilli felt even sadder. She came from a big family and she would miss every one of them when she was living in the city.

I'll be so lonely, she thought miserably.

Uncle Bernie was a great artist and as usual he was sitting on the front verandah painting when they arrived. Some of the paintings were about his country, some of them were just for fun, and others were things he had seen in his dreams.

'Oh that's wonderful!' Lilli cried when she

saw his latest one.

It was full of mango trees with bright golden fruit and red shrubs with rainbow birds perched in them.

'Thank you, bub,' Uncle Bernie smiled.

'That tree looks just like the one at Nan's place!' Lilli said. 'But what's that hidden in the shadows under the tree, Unc?'

Uncle Bernie chuckled. 'That's a little creature who visited me in my dreams, bub. He's a dingo cat and he lives inside that mango tree. I've painted him just for you. When you move to the city, he's going to take care of you!'

Lilli felt excited. *A dingo cat*, she thought in wonder, *a little creature to look after me in the city. Maybe I won't be so lonely after all!*

PACKiNG UP

Lilli tearfully kissed Nan goodbye then went to her room to pack all her things into the small suitcase her mum had given her.

'What are you doing Lilli Pilli?' Fatty Phil demanded, as he barged right in. 'Aw, you're not crying are you?'

Lilli spun around angrily. 'Don't call me Lilli Pilli!'

Just because her brother was excited about moving to the city, he expected her to be too.

'I have to pack my stuff,' she snapped crossly. 'Now go away!'

'How about I call you Grumpy Pilli?' he joked.

Lilli threw a pink teddy at him.

Fatty ducked, then darted out the door yelling, 'Dad said to tell you dinner's ready, Grumpy Pilli!'

Lilli felt so mad she almost chased after him, but then something quick and shadowy flitted across her desk.

What was that? she wondered. She looked again, but there was nothing there.

'Lilli!' her dad called. 'Come and have dinner. It's our last meal before we hit the Big Smoke, so it's yummy fish and chips.'

Lilli loved fish and chips but she felt too upset to eat much. Fatty Phil didn't mind — he gobbled down her dinner too. After dinner Lilli finished packing then turned out the light and went to bed early. She was nearly asleep when she heard a scrabbling sound under her desk. Lilli sat up. A pair of small glowing green eyes blinked at her in the half-light. The creature, which was darker than the shadows in the room, climbed onto her desk and sniffed the air. Then it slipped over to her dressing table and looked at itself in the big mirror. It was such a strange thing to do, Lilli almost laughed.

All of a sudden the creature grew so large it was as big as the mirror. Then it turned sideways and it was so thin it looked like a flat sheet of black paper. With a satisfied air, it floated down from the dressing table and

slid into Lilli's open suitcase. Lilli watched in astonishment as it folded itself under her clothes. Then two green eyes blinked at her and vanished.

What is it? wondered Lilli.

She was too scared to touch the suitcase, let alone pull everything out. She tugged the blanket over her head and closed her eyes. *Maybe I'm dreaming,* she thought. *Maybe I'm really asleep and this is all a dream.*

When Lilli woke the next day she remembered everything that had happened. Bravely she checked her suitcase. It was filled with her clothes and special things, but there was nothing else in there.

I must have imagined it, she thought.

She zipped up her suitcase and carried it out to the car, where her dad squeezed it into the boot.

'The Big Smoke's waiting for us,' he said cheerfully. 'It's time to hit the road!'

THE CITY

The new house in the city wasn't as bad as Lilli
had imagined it might be. In the back garden
there was a huge pepper tree that reminded
Lilli of Nan's big mango tree at home. Four
young boys were in the garden next door.
Instead of helping with the unpacking, Fatty
Phil leaned over the side fence and started
joking with them.

Who lives on the other side of our house?
Lilli wondered. *Is it a girl my age?*

As Lilli watched, an elderly lady stepped
out onto the front porch. When she saw
Lilli she smiled and waved. Lilli waved back
politely, but she was disappointed. It was

going to be harder for her to make friends
than Fatty Phil.

'Can I have the room that looks out over the
pepper tree?' Lilli asked her mum.

It wasn't a lovely mango tree, but it was
big enough to sit under and she knew that
whenever she looked at it she would think of
Nan.

'Of course you can!' Mum replied.

It took hours to unpack and organise the
house, but by the time they were finished,
everything looked really nice.

Almost like home, thought Lilli in surprise.

Then her dad came bustling in with dinner.
'We've all been working hard, so I thought
we could do with an early tea to celebrate our
first night in our new home.'

It was chicken and chips!

'We can't have takeaway every night,'
said Mum. 'It's too expensive. Tomorrow night
we'll cook.'

Lilli felt much hungrier than she had the night before, so when Fatty Phil greedily eyed her plate, she moved it away. It was a great feed.

After dinner, Lilli vanished into her bedroom to finish off the last bit of tidying up. Unlike Fatty Phil, she liked to have a place for everything and there were still a few special things in her suitcase she needed to put away. She lined up her pink teddy, her jewellery box, her favourite books and some shells she'd collected on a shelf near the window. Then she hung her best dress and two school shirts in her new wardrobe. The suitcase should have been empty, but when she went to close it she saw a black scarf lying in the bottom.

'This isn't mine!' she said out loud as she picked it up. It was soft and silky, almost like fur. It reminded Lilli of something, but she didn't know what. Suddenly the fur twitched.

'Arrgh!' Lilli screamed, dropping it in

fright and falling backwards onto her bed.

She watched in horror as the thing grew large and hairy. A pink mouth with razor sharp teeth appeared, then two sparkling green eyes blinked up at her.

'Hello Lilli!' a small voice said.

It was the creature from the night before. It looked like a cross between a cat and a dog, with its long pointed ears and dingo tail.

'What are you? What do you want?' Lilli demanded in fright.

The creature laughed and licked its paw. 'Don't you remember me? I was in your Uncle

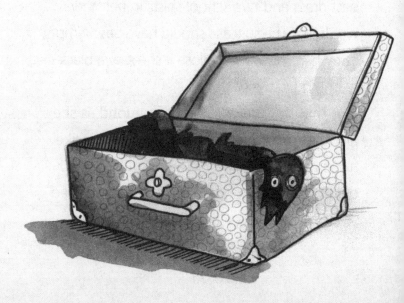

Bernie's painting! I've come to look after you for a while.'

Lilli didn't know what to think. What if it was something horrible and it was trying to trick her?

'I'll tell Mum and Dad about you!' she warned.

The creature grinned. 'No one can see or hear me except you!'

Then it pressed itself against the pale blue wall and, turning itself the same colour, disappeared completely.

Great, thought Lilli. *What do I do now?*

SHADOW

Lilli ran her hand over the wall where the creature had disappeared. The plaster felt smooth and cool — there was nothing there.

'Where has it gone?' she muttered.

She moved her hand further along the wall and stopped on a spot where the plaster felt warm. A dark furry outline began to appear.

Suddenly the creature shot out of the wall and jumped onto Lilli's bed laughing.

Despite her fear, Lilli laughed too. Then she blurted out. 'You're just like a shadow. One minute you're there, the next you're gone, and you can change shape and colour too.'

Shadow stretched happily across Lilli's pillow. 'Shadow boy — that's what Nan calls me,' he said. 'You can call me Shadow, too, if you like.'

'*My* Nan?' said Lilli.

'Of course your Nan,' said Shadow.

He really must be the dingo cat, thought Lilli.

'It's still light outside,' said Shadow. 'Let's play in the tree house.'

Lilli looked out at the gigantic pepper tree.

Shadow was right, there was a cubby hidden away in the leafy branches, and running down one side of the tree was a narrow wooden ladder.

Why didn't I notice that before? thought Lilli in surprise.

As Lilli climbed the tree, Shadow streaked past saying, 'Let's play hide and seek!'

He disappeared into the tree trunk and Lilli heard a muffled, 'Guess where I am?'

'How am I supposed to do that?' groaned Lilli, but Shadow just giggled.

Then she remembered what she had done with the wall. She climbed a bit higher and pressed her hand to the trunk, moving it over the rough bark until she found a warm spot. 'Found you!' she cried.

Shadow popped out all black and furry and gave her a hug. It felt like she was hugging a warm black teddy bear.

They sat together in the tree house talking.

'I have to go to school tomorrow,' sighed Lilli. 'I won't know anyone there and the other girls might not like me.'

She felt miserable just thinking about it.

'I'll come with you,' Shadow said. 'I'll make myself as small as a guinea pig and sit in your backpack.'

'Then I can come and say hello to you at lunch and recess,' said Lilli, delighted.

Starting at a new school didn't seem so bad now, not with a friend like Shadow.

STARTING SCHOOL

Baymarra Primary was only three blocks away from Lilli's new house. The boys next door — Mike, Jason, Tim and Spencer — walked with her and Fatty Phil. They seemed okay and her brother got on pretty well with them, especially Jason, who was the same age. Lilli hoped it wouldn't be long before she made some new friends too.

Lilli liked her new teacher Mrs Jones. She was nice and friendly and really interested to hear about the small town Lilli had come from. There were thirty children in the class, and about half of them were girls, so Lilli hoped that at least one of them might like her.

Before recess Mrs Jones gave the students free time to do something that interested them, like drawing, writing a story or reading a book. Lilli chose a book, and carried it to the large table at the back of the classroom. But as soon as she sat down a girl came up and said, 'That's my favourite book.'

Lilli didn't want to get into a fight on her first day, so she stood up to put the book back. But the other girl smiled and said, 'I'm

Alice. Don't you want to read it with me?'

Lilli realised that the girl was being nice to her, not mean.

'I'm Lilli. Do you like stories?'

Alice nodded. 'I love them. But I'm not very good at reading,' she added in a whisper, 'that's why I like doing it with someone else.'

Lilli sat with Alice and together they read the book.

'Do you want to have lunch with me?' Alice asked.

Lilli nodded. She liked Alice. She couldn't believe she had made a friend so quickly on her first day at school.

Lilli hadn't forgotten about Shadow, though. When Alice went to get a drink at the water fountain, Lilli opened her backpack and said hello to Shadow. 'Are you okay?' she asked.

'Of course I'm okay!' Shadow said. 'I like Alice too!'

Lilli gasped. 'How did you know I'd made a friend?'

'I sneaked into the wall of the classroom and watched you,' he grinned.

'Lilli,' Alice called suddenly, 'the bell's ringing. It's time to go back inside.'

'I'll see you at the end of the day,' said Lilli to Shadow. 'And no more sneaking!'

'Who were you talking to?' Alice asked, as they walked back to their classroom.

Lilli shook her head. 'No one.'

Alice looked disappointed. 'If I tell you a secret will you promise not to tell anyone?'

Lilli nodded.

'I only started at this school last year. When I first came here I didn't know anyone, so I used to bring my favourite teddy bear. I hid him in my backpack and talked to him at lunchtime. Does that sound weird?'

Lilli laughed. 'That's not weird at all.' Shadow was much stranger than a teddy!

Lilli felt light-hearted when she sat down for the afternoon's lessons. Alice was going to be a very understanding friend.

THE PROBLEM WiTH NAN

That night Lilli rang Nan for the first time.

'Guess what Nan, Uncle Bernie gave me a dingo cat called Shadow and he's my friend. He says he knows you.'

'Oh that's wonderful!' said Nan. 'I certainly know Shadow. I'm glad he arrived safely.'

'And I made a friend at school today, her name is Alice.'

Nan chuckled. 'I'm so happy to hear you're doing well. I was worried about you, but now I see I didn't have to worry at all.'

'I was worried about me too, Nan,' Lilli said, 'but this place is okay. I'd still rather be home with you though.'

'We can look forward to the school holidays. I'll save you some mangoes.'

At first Lilli rang Nan a lot, but as time went on she became so busy with Shadow and Alice and school that she didn't call as often. She knew Nan didn't mind. She was always cheerful when Lilli rang and was very happy that she was enjoying her life in the city.

But one afternoon after school her mum said, 'Lilli, I have some bad news. Your grandmother isn't feeling very well. Do you think you could give her a ring tonight?'

Lilli felt guilty. It had been more than a month since she last rang.

'There's nothing wrong with me but old age,' Nan said, when Lilli spoke to her on the phone, but her voice sounded weak and wobbly.

Lilli wished that old age was just like a

little wart that you could put medicine on and make it go away, but she knew it wasn't.

What can I do? she wondered that night as she lay on her bed. *How can I help Nan?*

Just then Shadow popped out of the wall where he had been hiding. It was his favourite place, but Lilli didn't feel like hunting for him tonight. She felt too worried about Nan.

'What's wrong?' he asked, sliding onto the end of her bed.

'Nan's not well,' said Lilli.

Shadow's furry face fell.

'Are you happy here, Lilli?' he asked after a little while.

Lilli thought for a moment then said, 'I didn't think I would be, but I am. I'm looking forward to the holidays though, so I can see the rest of my family again, especially Nan.'

'I think it's time I went home,' said Shadow. 'Then I can look after Nan for you. And besides, I miss my mango tree.'

GOODBYE SHADOW

Lilli rang Nan the next morning. 'Guess what, Nan? Shadow is coming home.'

'Oh no Lilli,' said Nan. 'I want him to stay in the city and look after you.'

'He doesn't need to look after me anymore, Nan. I'm all right now, I really am. Shadow needs to look after you. He said it's his job.'

'He said that?' Nan asked in surprise.

'Yes, he did. But I don't know how to send him back.'

'Oh it's not too hard,' said Nan. Her voice sounded stronger now, almost excited. 'When it's dark you'll need to light a fire, make sure the wind is blowing towards home. Shadow can come back on the fire smoke. You must talk to your parents, explain the situation to them and they'll help you do it safely.'

'But will they believe me when I tell them about Shadow?'

'Of course they will! When your mother was a little girl he looked after her too.'

Shadow must be really old, thought Lilli.

That evening Mum and Dad were only too glad to help.

'Can you test the wind, Dad?' asked Lilli. 'Nan said it has to be blowing towards home.'

'Sure can,' he said.

'Here's some dry kindling,' said her mum. 'But I really think it's you who needs to do the sending Lilli, because it's you he is attached to. We'll help you, but you should light the fire, and you must send him home.'

When everything was ready, and Dad was standing by with the hose to keep an eye on things, Lilli hugged Shadow one last time. 'I'll really miss you!' she said.

'I'll never forget you Lilli,' said Shadow. 'And when you come home on the holidays you can visit me in the mango tree.'

'You'll take care of Nan for me, won't you?'

'Of course! Now, help me ride the smoke, Lilli!'

Lilli watched fascinated as Shadow grew thinner and thinner until he was like a fine black scarf. Then she bent down and picked him up, gave him a quick kiss and gently flung him high into the smoke. For a moment, Shadow hovered in the smoky sky. Lilli saw his glowing green eyes blink at her once, then twice, as if to say goodbye. Then he twisted and turned, drifting higher and higher. A gust of wind suddenly swooped him up and Shadow sped off like a night bird flying home.

SOMETHING IN THE MAIL

The next morning the phone rang very early. It was Nan.

'He's here,' she told Lilli happily. 'He's back in the mango tree and he's busy telling me all about your life in the city.'

Lilli laughed with relief. She had been worried about him.

'I'm so glad he arrived safely, Nan!'

'It's wonderful to have him back. Thank you Lilli, you did a good job of sending him home.'

Lilli couldn't believe how strong and well Nan sounded.

'I really missed him,' Nan admitted. 'He's lived in that tree for such a long time and we've had a lot of little talks over the years. But Lilli, when I knew you were moving to the city I asked your Uncle Bernie to let Shadow enter his dreams so he could paint him, and then I knew it would be possible for Shadow to travel with you and look after you.'

So Nan had been behind everything all along!

'Shadow is very special, Nan, and I loved

having him with me, but now I'm happy he's home where he belongs.'

'I am too. And guess what? Maybe there is a cure for old age after all, because I'm feeling a lot better!'

Lilli laughed.

'I've put something in the mail for you, Lilli. So you won't forget Shadow. It will help you to remember home too, until you come up on the holidays.'

'Thank you, Nan!' said Lilli.

What could it be? she wondered.

A week later the postman delivered a long post office tube to Lilli's house.

'What on earth has Nan sent me?' Lilli asked, when her mum brought it into her room.

'Why don't you open it and find out?'

Lilli undid the tape, then popped the lid off the tube. She reached her hand inside and pulled out a rolled up piece of white material.

When she unrolled it she saw that it was
Uncle Bernie's painting.

Lilli smiled with happiness. The painting
was bright and beautiful, filled with mango
trees with bright golden fruit and red shrubs
with rainbow birds. And hiding in the shadows
near the mango tree from Nan's house, was
a shadowy animal. It was bigger than a cat,
about the size of an average dog. But it was
neither a cat nor a dog. It had a pink mouth
with razor sharp teeth and glowing green eyes
and it was smiling at her.

'Shadow!' Lilli whispered.

Lilli and Shadow in Trouble

LAURA DUDGEON AND
SABRINA DUDGEON-SWIFT

LiLLi's HOLIDAY

'Bye, Lilli, I'm going to miss you,' said Lilli's best friend, Alice.

Lilli was going to miss Alice, too, but she was really looking forward to spending the school holidays with her grandmother. She was also looking forward to getting away from the hustle and bustle of city life and being with her big extended family in her home country again.

The girls hugged a last goodbye and Alice gave Lilli an envelope.

'Don't open it until you are back at your Nan's house,' Alice whispered, as Lilli got into the car.

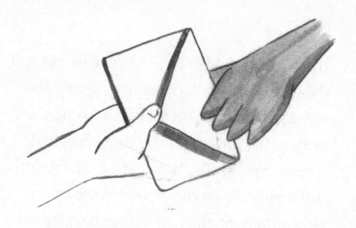

As they drove away Lilli leaned out the car window waving goodbye, goodbye, goodbye, until she couldn't see Alice anymore.

'What's the big deal — it's not like you'll never see each other again!' said Phil, rolling his eyes. Lilli glared crossly at her brother and ignored him.

Lilli thought over her first year in the city. She had made lots of friends and liked most of her subjects, especially writing and art. She was going to miss school and her new home, but tomorrow was the day she had been waiting all year for — she couldn't wait to see Nan again, and another special secret someone!

The next day the family — Mum, Dad, Lilli and Phil — flew up north. When they landed the air was dry and hot. As they walked into the terminal Lilli was smothered with kisses and cuddles from her big family. She laughed with excitement. Lilli looked around as she made her way through the crowd, searching for one person in particular — Nan.

'Lilli girl!' Nan shouted.

'Nan!' Lilli yelled, and she ran to Nan for a big hug.

As Nan squeezed her, Lilli felt Nan's black fluffy scarf tickle her nose.

Nan smiled her cheeky grin and Lilli felt a surge of happiness. She knew exactly what that black scarf was!

After they got their bags from the conveyor belt, Uncle Bernie herded everyone into a minivan and they drove through the small town. Lilli would be staying with Nan on her own while Mum, Dad and Phil would be staying with Uncle Bernie and his family. Lilli was so happy. She loved her Nan most of all and this holiday was going to be just like old times.

BACK WITH SHADOW

When Lilli opened the creaky old door at Nan's house, she realised just how much she had missed being there. Lilli went straight to the bedroom. Taking a deep breath she sat down on the bed with her back snug to the wall. She started to count to herself, waiting for something to happen. She closed her eyes and suddenly she felt a warm spot behind her head.

'I knew you would be here,' she smiled. But when she turned to the wall — nothing was there. She felt something brush lightly around her ankles, smooth like silk. She looked down quickly but again, nothing was there.

Lilli listened and watched for the slightest sound or movement. She was waiting for Shadow, her magical dingo cat friend. Shadow could change shape, and disappear into hard surfaces like walls and tree trunks, which made him great fun to be with. Shadow lived in Nan's mango tree, but Nan had sent him south with Lilli to keep her company when she first moved to the city. Lilli had really missed him since he'd returned home.

Feeling disappointed when he didn't appear, Lilli started unpacking. When she got to the bottom of her suitcase she found a black scarf.

Lilli held the scarf, gazing at it with joy and expectation. It started to twitch and change from smooth to warm and furry. It wound around her hand and slid around her arm all the way up and across the back of her neck. It tickled and Lilli laughed as it twisted itself back down her other arm to her hand. It jumped off her hand like a little black rabbit and landed perfectly on the bed beside her. A black dingo cat rolled around in laughter.

'I got you again! I got you again, ha ha ...'

'Shadow!' Lilli exclaimed with joy, looking at his big sparkly green eyes. As soon as she saw those eyes all the memories of their adventures together in the city came flooding back.

Shadow jumped into Lilli's empty suitcase. 'What's this?' he asked, handing a little blue envelope to Lilli with the curl of his tail.

'Oh ... I totally forgot about that! My

friend Alice gave it to me and she told me to open it when I get here.'

Shadow leapt gracefully from the suitcase and wrapped himself around Lilli's neck, watching as she slowly opened the delicate blue envelope. It contained a beautiful ribbon bracelet with blue, white and light purple plaits held together with Alice's little lucky button. With the bracelet was a note that read:

Dear Lilli,

My mum said that the bush is
filled with dangerous things, so
I'm giving you my lucky button
so you don't hurt yourself on
your adventures.
Don't forget about me. ☺
From your best friend,
Alice xx

'That's a really good present,' said Shadow
and they smiled at each other. Lilli was so
happy that she had good friends like Shadow
and Alice.

SHADOW FADING

Before Lilli went to bed, she gazed out the window at the old mango tree where Shadow lived. Shadow was out in the moonlight, wandering around the yard and sniffing the damp air.

Nan came in to tuck Lilli into bed. She looked worried.

'What's wrong, Nan?' asked Lilli.

Nan hesitated, then replied, 'I'm worried about Shadow. He hasn't been going to the mango tree lately. And he isn't as black as he should be. I think he is fading. See if you can find out what's bothering him. He is acting very strangely and I can't work out why.'

Lilli was surprised. Shadow seemed exactly the same to her.

Shadow was a magical creature — a guardian spirit. Lilli didn't know how old he was, all she knew was that he had been around since long before she was born and had been a very special friend to Nan from when Nan was a young child.

'Don't worry, Nan,' she said. 'I'll have a close look tomorrow.'

Nan tucked Lilli into her bed and kissed her goodnight. As Lilli drifted into sleep she felt Shadow snuggle into bed and cuddle up around her feet.

Lilli stared at Shadow in the morning light. Shadow had changed.

'Shadow, what is happening? Your colour looks different, it's as if you are fading!' she gasped. Shadow was a dark grey and the edges of his ears were transparent. Lilli scooped him up in a hug, yelling for Nan.

Nan came bustling into Lilli's bedroom.

'Nan,' Lilli cried, 'Shadow is fading!'

Nan sat on the bed and put her arms around Lilli and Shadow.

'Shadow, you really need to tell us what is happening. Why are you fading?' Nan asked gently, peering down at Shadow in Lilli's arms.

Shadow looked glum, his green eyes were not sparkling like they usually did — they looked a little faded as well.

Shadow sat on Lilli's lap, not speaking,
but as Lilli gently stroked his back, he seemed
comforted and finally he told Lilli and Nan
what was going on.

'I can't go back to the mango tree,'
Shadow said sadly.

'Why not?' asked Nan.

'Because something else is living there and
it won't let me in,' Shadow replied.

Nan was puzzled. In all the long years
that she had known Shadow, this had never
happened.

'What is the other thing living in the

mango tree?' Nan asked in her no-nonsense voice. 'If it's that cat that lives next door, I'll teach it quick smart not to mess with us and it can get out of our mango tree at once!'

'No, no, it is not a cat. It's a horrible nasty thing,' said Shadow as he burrowed closer to Lilli, turning himself into a scarf again and wrapping tightly around her shoulders.

'Oh, Nan, he is scared and shivering,' cried Lilli.

'Right!' said Nan. 'Let's go take a look at this thing in the mango tree. Things aren't allowed to just move in without my permission! Come with me, you two.'

THE MANGO TREE

Although Lilli was still worried and frightened, she felt much better. Nan was scary when she was cross. Nan would sort this uninvited guest out quick smart! Lilli scrambled out of bed and trotted after Nan. Nan grabbed her walking stick as she went out the back door. Lilli was still in her pyjamas with the big black scarf wrapped tightly around her shoulders and two round green eyes peered from the scarf.

They walked down the garden, past the red and gold hibiscus, until they stood in front of the mango tree. Nan's two old dogs followed them, looking at Lilli and Nan to see what they were up to.

The mango tree stood at the bottom of the backyard. It was a huge old tree and each season it gave the tastiest and juiciest mangoes in town. When the weather was hot, Nan would spread blankets out under the tree and sit in its cool shade. The mango tree was a part of their lives and it was like an old friend, but right now it looked scary. There was something different about the tree — it felt like a stranger.

'Okay, who is in our mango tree? Come out and show yourself!' Nan shouted at the tree.

There was silence. Nothing happened.

'This could take some time,' Nan said under her breath.

The watching dogs sat down and made themselves comfortable.

'Come out, I say!' shouted Nan and she whacked the trunk of the tree with her walking stick.

There was a yelp from the tree. Lilli,

Shadow and the dogs all jumped with
surprise. Then, they heard a creaking groan.

'Arrrgghh. Why are you whacking me, I
am just an old mango tree who gives you fruit
during mango season and shades you all year
round. You are a cruel old woman!'

'You are not the mango tree speaking!
Who are you?' asked Nan.

Nan might be old but she was not easily
fooled. She knew mango trees could not

speak. And if they could, it would be with nice ripe golden mango voices, not grey dry creaky groans like this voice. Nan waved her walking stick threateningly at the tree again.

'Leave me alone!' said the creaky voice.

'I don't think so!' said Nan. 'We need to talk.'

'Go away,' said the creaky voice. 'I'm not in the mood to do any talking with you! Nasty old woman!'

'That's it!' said Nan. 'I have had enough!' Nan turned on her heels and walked back to the verandah. Lilli and Shadow watched Nan as she grabbed the garden hose and walked back to the tree. Nan turned the hose on highest pressure and started spraying the tree from top to toe.

They heard a great loud yelp from the tree, and the creaky voice again, 'Okay, okay, I am not the mango. I am Glog.'

'Show yourself, Glog,' commanded Nan.

GLOG

Everything was quiet. Nan stood stiffly leaning on her walking stick, Lilli had her arms around Nan and Shadow had the whole of himself around Lilli. The dogs sat with ears pricked up, waiting. It was like everything was frozen.

Slowly, thin smoke curled from the bark of the mango tree. More and more smoke came out, but it was strange, staying in the one place — real smoke would have blown away in the morning breeze. Gradually the smoke formed a body about Lilli's size. Lilli could make out a head and long thin grey gnarly arms and legs. Finally a nasty looking creature stood in front of the mango tree. It

had no hair and looked like a twisted old tree
stump. It stared at them with dry grey eyes
and hissed, 'I am Glog …'

Lilli ran behind Nan and the dogs ran
behind Lilli. Lilli felt Shadow bristle up around
her.

'Err, right, hello Glog. Why are you in our mango tree?' Nan said, rather bravely Lilli thought.

'Because I want to be. Who are you to even ask me that?' Glog snapped back rudely, twisting his long arms and legs around themselves.

'Well, this is our tree and Shadow lives in it. You will have to go away and find another place,' Nan said sternly.

Suddenly Glog changed to a dark, steely grey colour and he grew twice as big. His mouth opened to reveal long, razor-sharp teeth and he said in a very nasty voice, 'Go away and do not question why I am here again or else there will be trouble.'

Lilli and Shadow were very frightened. The dogs scuttled back to the verandah and hid under the swinging chair. But Nan just pointed her hose at Glog again and squirted the water straight in his face.

Then a strange thing happened. Glog

became smaller and smaller, and transparent around his edges. He started to cry.

'Wahhh, I don't have anywhere else to go!'

He didn't seem so scary now, and Lilli felt sorry for him — so did the dogs, who came back out to the garden and gave Glog a sympathetic sniff and lick. Poor Glog was bawling. Between sobs he told them how his mangrove tree on the mudflats near the sea had been chopped down to make way for the new town jetty.

'There there,' said Nan patting his rough, wood-like shoulder. 'Come and sit down under the mango tree and let's figure out what we can do. Lilli, fetch the blanket please.'

NAN'S GREAT IDEA

By the time Lilli spread the blanket out under the tree Glog had stopped crying. Nan sat everyone down in a circle: Lilli, Shadow, Glog and herself. The dogs became bored and went back to the verandah to their sleeping mats. Nan told Glog how Shadow needed the mango tree. She explained that the tree was his home — although he could go away for a time, in the end he needed to come back to it to strengthen himself. If he didn't, he would gradually fade away until he disappeared completely.

'You mean, Shadow would die, Nan?' gulped Lilli, grabbing Shadow in a fierce hug.

Nan nodded and gave Lilli a serious look. 'Yes.'

'I am going to fade away, too! Look at me. I am fading now! Look at my beautiful arms,' shrieked Glog holding out his grey twisted arms. They were transparent at the ends where his twisty little stick fingers were.

Nan calmed him down and told everyone to leave her be while she figured things out.

While Nan was thinking, Glog told Lilli and Shadow about his life in the mangrove swamp. Lilli was surprised to learn that the mangrove swamp was so important and that so many creatures lived there.

'Yes,' Glog said proudly, 'the mangrove forest also stops the beaches from being hurt during storms. My home was the oldest and biggest tree. We had been through many, many storms together …'

Remembering that his tree was gone made Glog sad again. Lilli patted his rough arms to comfort him and told him that Nan would

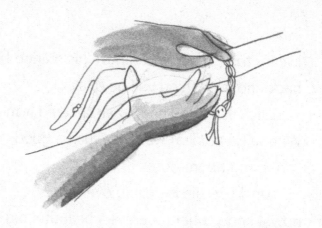

figure something out — she always did. Then Lilli had a good idea too. She took the ribbon bracelet from her wrist and tied it to Glog's arm.

'My best friend Alice gave this to me. It has a special lucky button on it so I am giving it to you so that you can be safe.'

Glog was very pleased and gave Lilli a scratchy hug.

'I have an idea!' Nan said at last. 'Lilli, go get the phone!'

When Nan had sorted things out she finally told them her idea.

'Right, Glog, you are fading and we have to get you to a mangrove tree that you can live in, then Shadow can have his mango tree back and everything will be okay.'

Lilli, Glog and Shadow all cheered Nan. What a great idea! Nan was such a good sorter and figure-outer.

'Uncle Bernie is driving over right now. I know where there is a beautiful big mangrove forest but it is way out bush, up the creek. Let's go in and have a wash and some breakfast before we go. Glog, can you make yourself small like Shadow?'

'Yes, of course I can. I can assume many forms,' replied Glog huffily.

After breakfast Lilli and Shadow came back to the mango tree for Glog and found an old branch lying under the mango tree. A creaky voice said, 'It's me.'

Lilli and Shadow giggled. Fortunately Glog was light, so Lilli hefted the branch over her shoulder and put it in the back of Uncle Bernie's ute.

It was a long drive and Lilli was happy she

was not bouncing around in the ute tray like
poor old Glog as they bumped their way to
Willi Creek. Finally, they arrived. There were
mangroves everywhere. Lilli had never seen
such a huge mangrove forest.

Lilli got out and spread the blanket on
some clean sand while Nan pulled out the
picnic basket with tea and snacks. Uncle
Bernie hauled the old tree branch from the
back of the ute.

'We should have a campfire with this. Lots of wood,' he joked.

The branch shrieked and twisted from his arms. Glog stood eyeing them balefully.

'I have been battered in that terrible car ride and now you want to burn me!'

Uncle Bernie and Nan laughed and told him it was a joke. Nan told Glog to walk amongst the trees with Shadow to see if there was a suitable one for him.

'With no one else living in there already,' she told him sternly.

FAREWELL GLOG

They drank their tea and waited. After a short time Glog reappeared. He had a big grin on his gnarly face. He told them that he'd found a new tree and was sure he was going to be very happy.

Lilli was pleased that Shadow was going to get his mango tree back, but she felt a bit sad about leaving Glog on his own in the mangroves. She secretly wished he could have stayed closer to Nan's house so that she could see him again. He really wasn't as cranky and mean as he made out to be.

Nan and Uncle Bernie packed up the picnic. It was time to say goodbye. They gave

Glog's thin grey hand a shake and wished him good luck. Nan told Glog not to pick on any other creatures and to try and make some friends.

Lilli thanked Glog for understanding that Shadow needed his mango tree back and wished him happier times in his new mangrove home.

She gave Glog a cuddle goodbye and headed for the car where Nan and Uncle Bernie were waiting.

'Lilli,' called Glog, 'I forgot to give you something.'

Glog opened his hand to reveal two small, almost identical, beautiful, glowing shells.

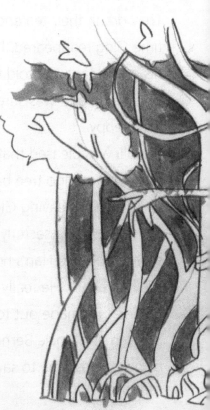

'What's this?' said Lilli.

'One shell is for you from the mangroves,' replied Glog, 'to keep you safe in your travels and as a reminder of the adventure that we all shared. The other shell is for your friend Alice, to replace her lucky button.'

'Thank you, Glog,' said Lilli and she waved a final goodbye.

That night Lilli snuggled up to Shadow in her bed.

'What an unusual day we have had, Shadow. As soon as we are together again life becomes an adventure. I am so glad that you are well now. I was going to write to Alice tonight and tell her about the bracelet, but she would never believe the story. Perhaps we could make new lucky bracelets with Glog's special shells.'

Lilli murmured on until she fell fast asleep. Shadow waited and cuddled Lilli again before he slowly moved from the bed to the window, gliding silently out to the back garden.

In the next bedroom, Nan looked out her window and in the bright moonlight of the back garden, she saw a black shadow slip past the sleeping dogs and cross the lawn to the old mango tree. It moved closer and then it vanished into the bark.

'Goodnight, Shadow,' Nan whispered, smiling as she lay down in her bed.

Beach Sports Car

DARLENE OXENHAM

A CRAZY IDEA

I live with my family in a caravan park in Useless
Loop — a crazy name for a crazy town. From
our caravan we look straight down over the
beach to the ocean. At night we can see the
lights of Shark Bay twinkling across the water.
I spend all my spare time on the beach —
swimming, collecting shells and fishing — so
when Dad said he wanted to get a beach sports
car, I was crazy with excitement.

'Imagine it, Annie,' Dad said, 'our own
sports car. And not just any sports car either,
but one we can drive along the beach! What
do you think?'

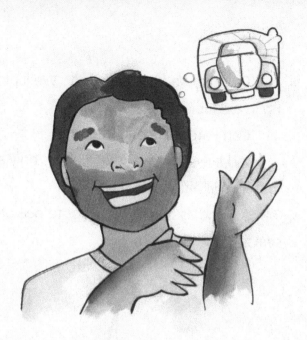

'I think it's great, Dad! But won't we get bogged?'

'I'll put big tyres on it to make it easier to drive over the sand.'

That sounded okay.

'But where are we going to get it from?'

Useless Loop was a long way from anywhere.

Dad grinned, 'It's already here!'

'What?' I squeaked. 'Where is it? Can I see it?'

'Calm down,' Dad laughed. 'We'll pick it up in a couple of days, okay?'

'Can Patches ride in it too?'

Dad eyed my little dog. He was only a pup and he still had accidents.

'As long as he promises not to pee on the seats.'

'Woof! Woof!' barked Patches.

WAITING FOR DAD

I can't wait!

We're picking up our beach sports car when Dad gets home from work today. Will it be sleek and low? What colour will it be? Will it have speed stripes running along the sides? How many of my friends will fit in it, and how fast will it go?

'How much longer before Dad gets home, Mum?'

'That's the tenth time you've asked me, Annie. I'll never get these biscuits done! Why don't you go outside and play with Patches? Then you can keep watch for your father.'

'Good idea. Come on, boy!'

Patches whined and licked his lips. There was a lovely cooking smell in the caravan. I think he was hoping for a treat.

'Off you go Patches!' ordered Mum.

His tail drooped and he followed me out.

'I'll get you a biscuit later,' I told him. Then I picked up his old tennis ball.

Playing a game would take his mind off Mum's biscuits and mine off our new car.

'Fetch,' I cried, and threw the ball as hard as I could.

Patches zoomed after it with a little wag in his tail.

BEEP BEEP

Dad!

I jumped up and down and waved my arms in the air. 'Dad! Dad! Over here!'

'Are you ready to go pick up our new car, Annie?' he bellowed, as he drove up the dirt track leading to our caravan.

'I've been ready forever!' I screamed.

THAT'S NOT A SPORTS CAR!

Dad parked the car and asked, 'Is your mother coming?'

I shook my head. 'She's making biscuits.'

Mum appeared in the doorway of the caravan. 'Just make sure it's all there!' she warned. Dad had once bought a fan with no blades.

Patches skidded up with his slobbery ball in his mouth.

'The dog can come, but not the ball,' said Dad.

I pulled the slimy thing out of Patches' mouth and threw it in an empty fishing bucket.

We climbed into the car and took off in a swirl of dust.

'Where are we going, Dad?' There was no car yard in Useless Loop.

'Red's place.'

Red was one of Dad's mates. His real name was Andrew, but everyone called him Red because of his red hair and sunburnt skin.

'Is the sports car there?'

'Sure is!'

It couldn't be that bad then. Red loved tinkering with cars.

Dad grinned. 'And from what I've heard Annie, she's a real beauty!'

When we pulled into the drive of Red's place he sang out, 'Hello little lady.'

'Hello Red!' I yelled, jumping out of the car with Patches.

'Hello Patches,' Red said, giving him a pat.

'Woof! Woof!' barked Patches.

'He's telling you we're here to pick up the car,' I grinned.

'Just don't let him drive it,' Red joked. 'He looks too young to me.'

I couldn't wait any longer. 'Where is it, Red?' I asked.

'Right there,' said Red, pointing to a small car covered with an old bit of canvas.

'You've got a smart dad, Annie,' Red said, as he whipped the canvas off. 'I never would have thought of turning this old bomb into a sports car.'

I stared at the battered, old Volkswagen in horror.

'That's not a sports car!'

A SURPRISE FOR MUM

We had to tow the car home.

I hoped none of my friends guessed the wreck we were dragging behind us was the sports car I'd been bragging about.

Dad sensed my disappointment. 'You have to use your imagination, Annie.'

'I can imagine it at the rubbish tip!'

'Come on Annie, you tell me what you'd like the car to look like and I'll make your dreams come true.'

Don't get sucked in, I told myself. But I did.

'It should be red and shiny with a white speed stripe running along the sides and no

roof. Plus, it would really help if the engine
worked.'

'Done,' said Dad. 'And you're going to
help me!'

I hadn't counted on that.

We parked the car in a shed near our
caravan and went in to see Mum. Mum
wanted to have a look at it straight away, but
Dad told her I wanted it to be a surprise.

He knew if Mum saw the old Volkswagen
now, she'd make him tow it to the tip.

'Come on, Annie,' Dad said, after he had polished off a whole plate of biscuits. 'We've got a weekend of work ahead of us.'

Dad locked the shed doors behind us, so Mum couldn't peek in. The car really was a bomb. Before I could stop him, Patches cocked his back leg on the rear wheel and peed. He didn't think it was too good either!

'Maybe we should start with the engine, Dad.'

'Good idea, Annie. I'll make a mechanic of you yet.'

Dad crawled under the car and asked me to pass him a screwdriver.

When I gave him the smallest one he grumbled. 'Wrong size! Open the second set and pass me the biggest one.'

I did as he asked, then said, 'Does it even have an engine?'

He laughed. 'I don't think there's too much wrong with her. Why don't you crawl under

here and have a look with me?'

Actually, that sounded kind of interesting.
I'd never looked under a car before.

I joined Dad in the dirt and he spent
the next few hours explaining what all the
different parts were and how cars worked.

Then Mum banged loudly on the shed door. 'Dinner's ready!'

'Time to call it quits for the day,' Dad sighed. 'I tell you what Annie, she'll be worth a fortune when we've finished. I bet you'll have dreams about her tonight.'

More like nightmares! How was I going to explain to my friends that we didn't have a sports car after all?

MAKING A SPORTS CAR

All day Saturday we worked on the car. By tea time I was covered in dirt and grease and oil, but I was also super happy. When Dad put the key in the ignition, the engine actually revved smoothly.

'She's purring like a Rolls Royce,' Dad laughed.

'Woof! Woof!' barked Patches, jumping around in the back seat. Even he was starting to like it now.

'We'll have to be up early tomorrow,' Dad said. 'It'll take me hours to cut off the roof with a pair of scissors.'

I almost believed him, but then I realised he was just teasing.

'Dad!' I yelled, punching him. 'But how are you going to get the roof off?'

'Red's coming over, he's got the right equipment. He's going to help us spray paint it too.'

That was good. Red knew a lot more about doing up cars than Dad did.

When the sun rose, so did we. Red was already parked near the shed, waiting for us to let him in.

'I can't believe you fixed the engine,' he said to Dad. 'I thought it was blown for sure.'

Then Red whipped out his welding gear. He was going to use his mean looking cutting torch on the roof.

'I want to keep the windscreen,' said Dad, 'but the side windows and the back can go.'

That's good, I thought, then the wind won't blow bugs in our teeth as we drive along.

'Right!' said Red. 'The trick will be cutting

all that away without cracking the glass in the front windscreen.'

There was a great whooshing and hissing sound as he turned the machine on. Sparks flew everywhere when he began cutting the metal. Patches ran outside, frightened.

'Er, I think I'll wait outside too.'

Before my eardrums burst!

THE PAINT JOB

Even outside the noise was deafening.
Everyone in the caravan park would be up
early this morning and it was all because of
Dad and Red. The noise went on for ages,
then there was a sudden SCREECH! BANG!
SMASH!

I rushed into the shed with Patches to see
what was happening.

Uh oh! The roof of the car was on the
ground and the glass in the side windows
was shattered into a thousand tiny pieces. But
luckily the windscreen was okay. Dad and Red
were grinning at the new open-top sports car.

'Come on Annie,' said Dad, 'you can help

us tape things up. 'It's time for the paint job.'

Wow! Things were happening really fast now.

Red had brought some paint with him that he'd found at the local tip. It was a glossy bright red. He had a small tin of white paint too, so it looked like I'd get my racing stripes.

It took all day to paint the car and by the time we went inside for dinner, it was dark. Mum wanted to grab a torch and look at it straight away, but Dad wouldn't let her.

'It's Annie's surprise,' he said. 'Don't spoil it for her. She'll show it to you in the morning, won't you Annie?'

I nodded.

The car was looking a lot better now, but the tyres were still wrong. They were skinny, one of them was flat and there was no spare.

Really, it was only half a sports car.

A TEST DRIVE

Early the next morning when I led Mum out to the shed, the doors were already open.

Patches poked his head out. 'Woof!' he barked, as if to say, 'What took you so long?'

Dad poked his head out too. 'About time, I thought you two were never going to get up.'

Mum smiled with delight when she saw the car. It was sleek and shiny and Dad had put four big fat new tyres on it. Now it really did look like a sports car!

'Time for a test drive!' he said.

We jumped in and Dad headed for the road that winds down to the beach.

'This is the real test, Annie,' he said, as he turned towards the sand dunes. 'Is it a beach sports car or not?'

I crossed my fingers and hoped we wouldn't get bogged — and we didn't! The car zipped through the dunes like a champion water skier.

'It works!' I cheered. 'It really works!

Then Dad drove down to the ocean and we flew along the harder stretch of sand near the water. It was brilliant!

'This looks like a good spot,' Dad said as he pulled up onto a flat stretch of rock overlooking the sea. Then he reached his arm over his side of the car and pulled up three fishing rods.

'I've got a little gadget just here,' he said proudly, 'for the rods to click into.'

I leaned over the side. He did too. It was a great way to carry rods.

'But that's not all,' he said, jumping out.

He opened the boot and passed me the bait
and bucket. Then he pulled out a beach
umbrella, opened the front passenger door
and leaned over Mum. I hadn't noticed before,
but fixed into the floor, between the seats,
was a metal tube. Dad stuck the umbrella in,
then popped it open. 'We can fish from the
car and be in the shade at the same time!'

Mum threw back her head and laughed.
So did I.

THE BEACH SPORTS CAR

After breakfast, Dad drove me to school and
Patches came too.

He loved the way the wind blew in his face
in our beach sports car. He opened his mouth
and his cheeks filled with air. Then he ran
from side to side in the back seat looking at
everything we passed.

'Woof! Woof!' he barked, as we headed
down the street towards Useless Loop Primary.
'Woof! Woof!'

'Oh stop showing off, Patches!' I laughed.

All my friends were hanging out the front
of the school, like they normally do on a
Monday morning.

'Hey, everyone,' my best friend Brian yelled out. 'Look at Annie!'

Soon they were all calling out. 'Annie, Annie, where did you get the cool car from?'

'Wow, look at its tyres, I bet they'd go over anything!'

'And it's got racing stripes — how fast does it go Annie?'

When Dad parked the car, they all swarmed around us, asking if they could have a ride in it one day.

'Of course you can!' Dad said, 'but you'll have to take turns, it's only a small car after all.'

'But what kind of car is it?' Brian asked.

He was looking at the fishing rods hanging off the side and the round metal tubing poking up between the front seats.

'It's a Beach Sports Car!' I said smugly.

The school bell rang and everyone raced inside except Brian, who couldn't stop looking at the car.

As I climbed out Dad said, 'Hey Annie, it's a low tide tomorrow afternoon. How about you and Brian and me head down to the beach? We should be able to drive the car right out onto the ocean floor and get some really pretty shells.'

Brian looked like he couldn't believe his luck.

Dad tooted at us, then spun the sleek, shiny, speedy red car around and drove off.

'Your dad's so great!' Brian sighed, as we went inside.

'Do you reckon he could show my dad how to make a Beach Sports Car?'

A Cyclone is Coming!

DARLENE OXENHAM

POP'S WATER TRUCK

I wake with a fright to the sound of Patches barking madly outside my window. I pull the curtains back, open the window and look outside. Sure enough, Patches is right under my window looking up at me. I smile down at him and say, 'Okay, okay. I will take you for a walk.' He wags his tail at me as if to say, 'Hurry up, Annie. I have been waiting forever.'

I live with my parents in a caravan in a place called Useless Loop and I just love it. My grandparents and their youngest children — my aunt and uncles — live next to us on the bottom terrace. It may seem a bit strange to some people but my aunty and two of my uncles are only a couple of years older than me. I don't know how this has worked out, but I am really happy that it has because they are not only my relatives but they are great friends and fun to be around.

There are only about ten other kids my age in Useless Loop and we are all friends. During the holidays we do everything together. We go swimming at the beach. We go fishing off the jetty and collecting shells. We do lots of things!

But today I have a plan. Today I am going to visit my grandad who is in charge of carting

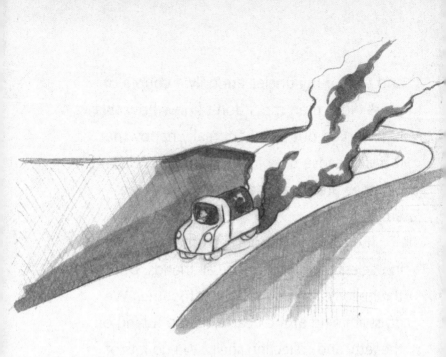

the water that we all use for drinking and cooking. It is a lovely warm sunny day and best of all it is school holidays, so I can do what I want.

'Come on, boy, let's go see Pop.'

'Woof,' replies Patches.

We walk up the caravan park terraces, looking at everything that is going on. Seagulls swoop in searching for scraps of food. Lizards scurry here and there on lizard business. Patches tries to chase a few but they always get away by running under rocks.

In the distance I can see dust on the road out of town. That means Pop is on his way back with a load of water. You can always tell when Pop is coming because of the cloud of dust stirred up by his truck.

We wait as Pop pulls in and swings the big hose over the top of the tank.

'Hello there little one, how are you today?' asks Pop.

'Good, Pop. We brought you an apple.'

'I am always pleased to see you, Bub, but I am especially pleased to see you when you have brought a snack for me.'

Pop releases a lever that pumps the water from the truck into the big water tank. As the water is pumping we sit and eat our apples.

'I'm thinking of going to the beach today, Pop,' I say.

Pop looks at the sky and then at the sea and says, 'I don't think you should. The sea looks a bit rough and the wind is getting up. Besides, your mum and dad will need your help to prepare.'

'Prepare for what?' I ask.

'The cyclone,' Pop replies. 'A cyclone is coming.'

PREPARING FOR THE CYCLONE

Well, Pop was right! Yesterday afternoon the wind started blowing and has not stopped blowing since. I have never been in a cyclone before. In fact, I'm not even sure what a cyclone really is.

'A cyclone is like a very big storm,' Dad explains. 'There is plenty of rain and the wind can blow hundreds of kilometres per hour and do lots and lots of damage.'

'Oh, that sounds scary, Dad!' I say.

Dad smiles. 'It can be a bit scary, but we need to think of it as an adventure and be prepared. For a start, I will go and pick up the scraper.'

'Why?' I ask.

'Because I am going to tie the caravan to it. The cyclone that's coming is pretty big — big enough to overturn a caravan. I need to tie it to something so heavy it can't move. I guarantee the caravan won't blow away if it is tied to the scraper.'

'That's for sure, Dad!'

'Come on, Annie, you can help me pick up any loose things like toys, brooms and bikes,' Mum says. 'We need to put everything away

116

so the wind doesn't blow it into our caravan or anyone else's. After that, we need to tape up the windows.'

'Why?' I ask.

'The glass may break in the cyclone,' explains Mum. 'It depends on how strong the winds are, but it's safer if we tape them. That way even if they do get broken they won't shatter into small pieces. The tape will hold them together. We need to leave the windows open a bit too, so that the pressure inside the caravan will be the same as it is outside.'

Wow, this is an adventure — scary but exciting!

While Dad is gone I walk over to Nan's caravan to see if they are preparing for the cyclone as well. As I step through the door I can hear Nan in the kitchen of the caravan, and I see my aunty — Joyce — and two uncles — Neville and Malcolm — playing cards at the table in the annexe.

Nan pops her head out of the caravan and calls, 'Hey sweetie, have you come for a visit?'

'I'm waiting for Dad to come back with the scraper and thought I would come and see what you were doing,' I reply.

'Well,' Nan says, 'I was just trying to get those lazybones,' she gestures to my aunt and uncles, 'to start cleaning up around here.'

I look over to where Joyce, Neville and Malcolm are playing cards and say, 'Come on then, I will help you until Dad gets back.'

As we are finishing the cleaning around Nan's caravan, I hear Dad call out, 'Do you want to help me tie down the caravan, Annie? All you have to do is catch the rope when I throw it to you.' I race back home to help.

In the end I have to catch three ropes. Each of the ropes is tied to a plastic-covered chain that Dad drags across the caravan and then ties securely to the scraper. There is no way our caravan is going to blow away!

WAITING FOR THE CYCLONE

We have tidied up everything. All my toys are stacked away. Nothing loose has been left lying around. All the cleaning has been done. I don't think there is anything else to do.

'Last-minute check,' Mum calls to Dad.

'Spare batteries for the radio,' she says.

'Check,' answers Dad.

'Full water containers.'

'Check.'

'Canned food.'

'Check.'

'Ice for esky and frozen food moved.'

'Check.'

'Matches and gas bottles.'

'Check.'

'Portable stove.'

'Check.'

'Sleeping bags.'

'Check.'

'First aid kit.'

'Check.'

So we have done everything that we need to do. Now all that's left is to wait for the cyclone to hit.

THE COUNTDOWN

Waiting for a cyclone is a scary time AND a boring time.

After lunch Mum, Dad and I play board games in our annexe. We have played one game of Monopoly and just finished Snakes and Ladders. I lost!

'When is the cyclone meant to get here, Dad?' I ask.

'The last radio broadcast estimated the cyclone would hit us late in the afternoon,' Dad replies.

I look at the clock and groan. It is only one o'clock so it could be hours before the cyclone gets here.

Mum puts my *Harry Potter and the Goblet of Fire* DVD on. This is my favourite Harry Potter movie and I must have watched it about ten times now. The movie is halfway through when suddenly the power goes off.

'Oh my god,' I yell. 'Does this mean the cyclone is here now?'

'Shh, be calm,' Dad says. 'The cyclone is not here yet. The power has been turned off as a safety measure.'

My heart is still pumping hard as I stand in the middle of our small kitchen, not really sure what to do with myself.

Mum reaches for my hand and says, 'Come and help me put out the torches and lamps ready for when it gets dark.'

Dad turns up

the radio to listen to the cyclone update.

'Residents of Denham and Useless Loop are warned that Cyclone Tessie is approximately two hours away. Cyclone Tessie is a category 3 cyclone with expected wind gusts of 150 kilometres per hour. Residents are urged to stay inside at all times and to ensure that loose materials are secured. Regular cyclone updates will be broadcast each hour.'

'Right. We need to do the final jobs now,' says Dad.

'But I thought that we had done them all,' I say.

'Not quite,' replies Dad.

OUR SAFE PLACE

In a cyclone everyone is told to identify the safest place in the home. Our safe place turns out to be the kitchen of our caravan. Dad explains that this is the safest place for us because we are protected by the seats along the wall of the caravan and by the kitchen cupboards, so we have a barrier between us and any stuff flying into the caravan.

Dad has put three mattresses on the kitchen floor and folded the table down and put a big double bed mattress on top as another layer of protection.

'If I tell you to hide, you have to quickly squeeze yourself under the kitchen table and stay there until Mum or I tell you that you can move,' Dad says.

This scares me a lot because there is only space for me under the table. I wonder what will happen to Mum and Dad but I don't say anything. I just nod.

I look at the clock on the wall.

'Dad, Mum, look — it's half past three. The cyclone will be here soon!'

I walk over to the window and look outside. In the sky I can see dark clouds gathering to block out the sun. It smells of rain.

Patches has made himself a nice little bed under the kitchen table and looks like he is settled in for the night. We spread out our sleeping bags and pillows and get comfortable. I hear the rain begin to fall lightly on the caravan.

Dad opens up a special box he has packed. In the box is my portable DVD player and several movies; there are five bottles of water,

candles, matches, some tins of tuna and other food, books, comics and crosswords, a deck of cards and other games.

'See — everything we need to weather a cyclone,' Dad says.

Mum opens her book and begins to read as Dad and I start our first game of cards. Outside the sky is darker and the rain is heavier. The wind has started to really blow. I can hear the annexe whipping backwards and forwards as the wind gusts push it in and out. The rain beats down hard on the caravan. Thud, thud, thud, thud, thud. It is getting scary now. Dad has to turn up the radio to hear what is being said.

'We interrupt this program with a news update. Cyclone Tessie is now passing over the townships of Denham and Useless Loop. Wind gusts have been recorded at 156 kilometres per hour. The cyclone is approximately 100 kilometres wide. Residents of Denham and Useless Loop are advised not to venture outside — that is, under no circumstances go outside. The cyclone is expected to take six hours to pass over Denham and Useless Loop.'

we interrupt this
program with a news
updat...

THE CYCLONE IS HERE!

Mum looks at me and sees how scared I am.

'Come and jump into bed next to me,' she says, 'We can read a comic together.'

Outside the wind is howling around the caravan. The annexe is flapping so much I worry the stakes will never hold.

'It is okay. Everything will be fine,' reassures Dad.

I look at the clock. This is going to go on for hours, I think in despair. I try to concentrate on my *Superman* comic, but after reading the same page five times I give up. I can't concentrate at all.

'Righto, everyone. I think we should have

an early dinner,' announces Mum.

We have chicken and corn soup which Dad heats up on the small gas burner, followed by tuna and salad sandwiches, then tinned peaches and ice-cream from the esky.

Patches pops his head out from under the table to get his dinner and then goes right back and immediately off to sleep. I wish I could do the same!

While we eat, the wind and rain get heavier and louder outside.

After dinner Dad suggests that I watch another movie with my headphones on. This is not so bad because all I can hear is the movie. As I watch I glance over at Mum and Dad several times. They have their heads together talking, but they don't look really worried.

If they are not worrying, I think, then I won't either. And I don't, until the movie finishes and I take my headphones off. The noise is incredible. The caravan is beginning to sway and shudder.

Dad looks at me and says, 'Don't be afraid. We are not going to blow away. Remember, we are tied to a twenty-tonne scraper. Not even this wind can drag us away from that. Choose another movie.'

Halfway through *Transformers*, Dad taps me on the shoulder and gestures for me to take the headphones off. When I do, all I can hear is … silence. No wind, no rain; and it is sunny! I cannot believe it. Dad takes me to the window so I can look outside. It is amazing. It is just like a nice normal day.

'This is the eye of the cyclone. Incredible, isn't it,' Dad says. 'The eye is at the centre of the cyclone and it is very calm — no wind, no rain. But you must not be fooled, because once this passes then the winds and rain are back again. So you must never go outside when the eye of the cyclone is passing.'

Dad and I watch until the sky begins to darken, a light rain starts falling and the wind gusts get stronger again. Soon the wind is once again howling and the rain pounding down on the caravan. The caravan is shaking so much it begins to make squeaking noises. It is like a giant hand is pushing against it.

I lie next to Mum again to read my comic. Mum is reading her book and Dad is doing a crossword and listening to the radio. This has been a very scary and exhausting day but there is no way I will be able to sleep tonight.

What will tomorrow bring?

AFTER THE STORM

We are all up early in the morning. I really
didn't think I would sleep last night, but I did. I
think that in a strange way the swaying of the
caravan actually helped me sleep!

Patches is desperate to go to the toilet and
we want to see what damage the cyclone has
done.

The first thing I notice when we walk
outside is all the broken branches and leaves.
They are everywhere. There is no wind or rain
but the ground is very muddy.

We walk around our caravan and annexe
but everything is fine and in its place.

'See — the scraper was a good idea,

wasn't it,' Dad says.

'Sure was, Dad!' I reply.

We walk over to Nan and Pop's to make
sure that everything is okay at their place. Nan
and Pop, and Joyce, Neville and Malcolm, join
us outside, and we stand together looking
at all the other caravans. Suddenly Malcolm
points and yells, 'Look at that!' We look in
the direction he is pointing and see a dinghy
leaned up against a caravan.

'Must have been blown off its trailer,' Pop
observes.

'Hey, I wonder what else has been blown
around,' says Joyce.

'Dad, can we go and have a look?' I plead.

Dad looks at Pop before he replies, and
Pop nods his consent.

'Yes, you can. But stay together and be
careful,' Dad instructs.

We all take off at a run. We wander
around for about an hour looking at all the
things that had been blown about. Some

people had forgotten about their bins and these had been blown over and all the rubbish thrown out. I see four seagulls land and begin to scavenge through the rubbish looking for juicy bits to eat.

Everyone in Useless Loop is out and looking at the damage caused by the cyclone.

'I think we have been lucky,' says Neville. 'Really there is not much damage and no one got hurt.'

Neville is right. It looks like one huge mess, but really it won't take too long to clean it all up. We are lucky. It's strange how last night I was so very scared and now today I feel excited. Everything is okay and it is a new day with new adventures to come.

BACK TO SCHOOL

'Who wants to tell news?' asks Mrs Frost, our teacher.

I slowly put my hand up.

'Annie, good. Thank you for being first,' says Mrs Frost.

'My news today is about the cyclone,' I begin. I hear a few groans around the class and someone whispers, 'Boring.'

I continue, ignoring the comments of my very rude friends.

'After the cyclone Joyce, Neville, Malcolm and I looked all over the caravan park to see what damage had been done. Then Malcolm

said why don't we go to the beach and so
we did and there were lots of things that we
found.'

I look at my aunt and uncles for help and
Malcolm starts wiggling and shaking his arms
around.

'Is there something you would like to
share, Malcolm?' asks Mrs Frost.

'Yes. We found an octopus,'
says Malcolm. He takes out a glass
jar and puts it on his desk. The kids
rush over to look at the octopus.

'Everyone, back to your own
seats NOW!' says Mrs Frost sternly.
'Annie, as you found these things
with Neville, Malcolm and Joyce, they can also
tell news with you. Go ahead.'

'We found a crab that had died,' I say. This
time Neville brings out a square tin container.
He opens the lid to reveal a greenie-blue crab
with a few missing legs.

'Children, stay where you are,' instructs

Mrs Frost before anyone can get up. 'Neville, pass it around so everyone can have a look.'

'We also found a flat tyre tube, a broken kite and a dead stingray which we didn't bring because it smelt bad,' I say, screwing up my nose as I remember it.

'But the best thing we found was a bottle.' I look at Joyce who is holding up a light-green bottle. 'It had a cork in the top and a message inside.'

Everyone is very excited.

'Did you read the message?'

'What did it say?'

'Who was it from?'

I look at Neville, Malcolm and Joyce and we all smile.

'Yes, we read the message,' I say. 'But *that* is another story,' I finish smugly and sit down.

There is silence.

'Have you finished telling your news now?' asks Mrs Frost curiously.

'Yes,' replies Neville.

'Ah, a mystery,' says Mrs Frost. 'Well, Tom, perhaps you would like to go next and tell us about how your annexe fell down?'

Everyone groans as Tom stands to tell his news about the cyclone.

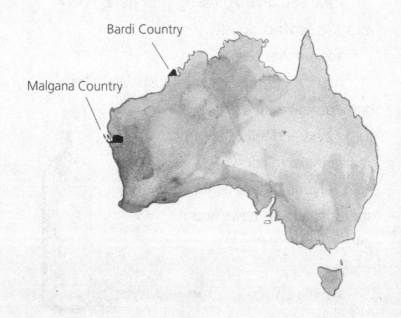
Bardi Country

Malgana Country

ABOUT THE AUTHORS

Laura Dudgeon was born in Darwin in 1993. Her country is the Kimberley and she is descended from the Bardi people from north of Broome and the Giga people in the East Kimberley. Laura's stories were inspired by her nana and based in her hometown of Darwin. Lilli's move from a country town to the city was based on Laura's own experience of moving with her mother from Darwin to the big city lights of Perth.

Pat Dudgeon is Laura's aunty. Like Laura, she was born in Darwin but in 1959. Her people are from Broome way in Western Australia. Pat was fortunate to grow up with her mother and grandmother who were great role models for her. Laura and Pat wrote their story thinking about their lovely grandmothers.

Sabrina Dudgeon-Swift is the eldest of four children; Laura is her littlest sister. Sabrina's people are from Broome, though she lived in Darwin before moving to Perth in 2001. Sabrina's childhood was spent in Darwin fishing from the banks where the mangrove trees grew and exploring the beaches and bushlands with her friends. Sabrina was fortunate to have her nana living close by. Sabrina's nana often told her stories of her adventures and mischief during her younger years.

Darlene Oxenham was born in Denham, Shark Bay. She is a Malgana woman and her country is around Shark Bay, between Geraldton and Carnarvon on the coast of Western Australia. Darlene's stories were inspired by her time living with her family in Useless Loop, a time of innocence and wonder that she values greatly to this day.

Darlene gives particular thanks to her grandparents, Maude and Stump, and makes special mention of her aunty Joyce and uncles Neville and Malcolm whose real names she used to give them full acknowledgement.

LIKE THESE STORIES? TRY:

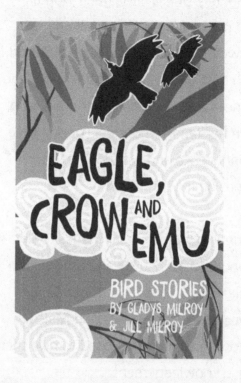

Birds who can't fly and snakes who can;
mistakes to be made and problems to be solved;
great enemies and even greater friends —
all this and more in three exciting stories full
of action, adventure and birds!

AVAILABLE NOW